I0570624

Velvet Cloth

Velvet Cloth

Poems Long and Short,
Stories, Essays, Plays,
and a Fantasy Novella

Ronald P. Fattibene

Epigraph Books
Rhinebeck, New York

Velvet Cloth: Poems Long and Short, Stories, Essays, Plays, and a Fantasy Novella © 2016 by Ronald P. Fattibene

All rights reserved. No part of this book may be used or reproduced in any manner without written permission from the author except in reviews and critical articles. Contact the publisher for information.

Library of Congress Control Number: 2016952963
ISBN: 978-1-944037-42-0

Book design by Colin Rolfe

Printed in the United States of America

Epigraph Books
22 East Market Street
Suite 304
Rhinebeck, NY 12572
(845) 876-4861
www.epigraphps.com

DEDICATED TO

SLEEPING CHILDREN

TABLE OF CONTENTS

INTRODUCTION

Authors think of their writings as their children. Produced with infinite care, shown to a few friends, and lovingly tucked away in some obscure file where they sleep undisturbed.

I came across one such file recently. It was entitled "Miscellaneous writings: poems, stories, essays, etc."

I felt it was time to wake them for public scrutiny. So here they are. Please be kind. They're fragile.

Velvet Cloth

They said
to me
Come
be free
When life was young
and green
And soar aloft
on velvet cloth
To taste of things unseen.
Did I build a cage
stage by stage
and clip the wings
so soft
to huddle here
in secret fear
that the dream
was lost?

April, 1960

"The River of Li"

On the magical, mystical
River of Li
We sailed our bamboo raft
Just you and me,
and ate leechee nuts
Under the Yin-Yang tree

Where the buffalo swim
to the isle of green
And the mist descends
almost unseen
On the craggy cliffs
just below Kwelien.

In my mind's eye
I still return
to that fabled land
of the fluted fern
Where the dragon
with the great humped back
sleeps neath the white tiered
castle on the mountain black.
And the eagle soars
through the misty glen
and the children play
in the Land of Fen.

Where furry men
with little feet
Trod the limestone
cobbled street
Underneath, between
pristine walls
they tend rock mushrooms
beside stone waterfalls

In what long forgotten dream
did I first see Kwelien?
Did the mountains rise
green and stark
above the fisherman's
tiny bark?
And split the sky
with jagged grace
to give the land
its lusterous face.

When I die, my spirit
will soar
And light upon
the Kwelien shore
Where I will sail
the Li
Evermore.

China, June 1983

THREE FEET HIGH
(for my children)

When they were young
One said to me
"Tell me Daddy
is that a tree?"
"No," said I
"It's just a sprout
but someday
it'll grow
and move
its limbs about."
"Will I do
that too,
grow big and tall?"
She smiled
from a face
pudgy and small.
"You will
my dear
but in my mind's eye
you'll always be
three feet high."

Her forehead
furrowed
deep in thought
her chin
all vanilla
from the
ice cream
I bought.
"That sounds funny.
What does it mean?"
"It means,"
I said
"that you'll
always be
if only
in a dream."

I came across
a photo
the other day
of two tiny girls
in bonnets of grey
riding a car
in a miniature
raceway
and I remembered
my words of yesterday.

They still
smile and
giggle
and peek
at me
across the
years
and in
my mind's eye
they've
always
been there
just
three feet high.

July, 1975

CLARISSA AND THE JUG-HANDLE CURVE

Clarissa threw a mean jug-handle curve.

And I don't mean a typical, tiny little swerve, but a gol danged, rip-snortin', rooty-tooty, big whopper of a throw.

Immediately upon leaving her hand the ball took a sharp left turn, rose in a giant arc, swept toward home plate, then dove with a whoosh over the tiniest sliver on the right side of the slab.

It was a sight to behold.

Clarissa had fallen from her toddler bed when she was three and had severely fractured her left arm. It dangled at a precarious-looking angle for the rest of her life. But it gave her the gift of her jug-handle curve.

And she loved to throw it! But the girls glared at her and the boys avoided her.

She tried out for the high school baseball team. Although coach McCoon whistled loudly as the ball whizzed through the air, he refused to let her play.

"The boys will all quit," he moaned. "But it is the most beautiful thing I've ever seen."

The fate stepped in. Eighteen-year-old Henry fell madly in love with Clarissa, and she with him. Henry wasn't looking at her arm; he was looking at the rest of her.

They married, had five kids, bunches of grandchildren—Clarissa had no idea how many—and a gazillion great grandchildren, as she liked to joke.

One night, when she was 92, she woke to unusually bright moonlight streaming through her bedroom window.

A luminous circle of light spotlighted the grass outside and seemed to beckon to her.

"I wonder," Clarissa mused. Gathering up her bloomers, she wrapped her nightshirt about her neck and crept down the creaky steps. Carefully she made her way through the old wood front door—also creaky—and into the blackness of night.

In her hand she held the baseball her great, great, great grandson Anson had given her. She paused momentarily in the circle of white light, luxuriating in the moment.

Clarissa raised her crooked left arm, and with a small sigh, she threw the small sphere toward the side of the barn. And there it was—in all its glory—the jug-handle curve.

She could still do it!

Clarissa leaped up and let out a loud Indian war whoop, then did a little jig in place.

Nobody knew or cared that she could still pitch the jug-handle curve at 92 years of age.

But she did.

September, 2012

DR. GREY

Dr. Sturdevarth Periwinkle-Grey was six feet, 11 inches tall, gaunt, bald, brilliant and a royal pain in the ass. His speech was unintelligible and he refused to repeat himself, scowling when questioned.

As he strode through the hospital corridor surrounded by interns, his head jerked above them like a bobble doll and his white coat flapped about his ungainly legs. His stethoscope swept majestically side to side and his adam's apple rose up and down. With every moving part in concert, he looked like a rare species of whooping crane fleeing his would-be captors.

"Ah," said Dr. Periwinkle-Grey after reading his first patient's chart during morning rounds. "Snitchelfraunt relekaposeosis. With complications due to alterisis remgleblete," he elaborated. We assumed a demeanor of intense concentration and nodded in collegial assent.

He looked earnestly at us, seeking a response to his diagnosis. "Ribbit," we said in unison. "Ribbit?" he questioned. Slowly a slight smile lightened his expression; then he began to laugh in acknowledgement. "Okay," he said, then moved on to the next patient.

August, 2011

THE ROCK GARDEN

One-person play; character: A LITTLE GIRL

Isn't this a beautiful rock garden? (arms outstretched) I love coming here.

I made it all myself, it started out as a hobby 100 million years ago. But as you can see, it kind of got out of hand.

I mean it's humongous, (stretches out her hands).

(Gestures right, left, in back and in front.) (Could turn about playfully with outstretched arms.)

It goes on as far as the eye can see. It's sort of—endless.

Well, you might guess that it's a lot of work (sigh), and I just can't get to all of it.

Take that corner over there. I have a nice big sun out there, so if I do it just right I should be able to come up with something really nice. You know, pretty and grows nice too. Then, when I look at it from time to time it'll give me pleasure.

(SHE stops, looks toward the audience.)

My problem was, I couldn't come up with the right thing to put there. So a while ago after working hard cleaning,

I decided to take a rest.... Over there, right near that big boulder.

(SHE indicates a box at stage right. SHE walks to the box, sits down and rests her forearms on her knees, folds her hands, and begins humming to herself, rocking back and forth. As SHE does so, SHE looks up and smiles.

I like humming. I don't sing too well so humming calms me and helps me think better.

Anyway, I'm sitting there, resting, rocking, humming and thinking about what to grow.

The sweat is just pouring down all over my face and reaching down between my legs on to the dirt and making mud. Without thinking I pick up a small rock and begin packing the mud around it.

(SHE reaches down, scoops up some imaginary mud and begins to pack it into the mud ball. The ball becomes larger and larger.)

Pretty soon before you know it, I got a pretty big mud ball. So I twist it and turn it and play with it till I get it good and round.

And then I spin it and my gosh there it is.

(SHE spins the imaginary globe and then places her index finger under the apex. She lengthens her arm—the ball spinning on it and eventually withdraws—indicating that the ball is in space spinning on its own).

Well, I'm looking at this spinning thing for quite a while.

And then one thing that struck me was how gosh-awful homely it was—I mean brown is brown and there are certainly prettier colors in the universe. For example, I'm pretty partial to blue or green—well anyway at first I made it all blue.

(Waves at the spinning ball)

I keep it that way for quite a while.

Then I added green. Big splotches of green, a little here and there.

(SHE points her finger at different parts of the ball.)

Not bad. Not bad.

(SHE cups her head in her hands, rocks back and forth humming.)

Needed something else but at first I didn't know what. One last touch and then it would be complete.

(SHE continues to rock, humming and a slow smile begins to come over her face.)

That's it, that's it.

(SHE reaches over and begins touching the globe at various points abruptly with her forefinger.)

Living things. Little amebas. In different colors of course.

So I make green ones, white ones, black ones, yellow ones.

(SHE keeps punching various parts of the globe with her forefinger.)

And they are so funny. They're running around like crazy bumping into one another and making an awful racket.

I started to laugh. I mean it was the most fun I had had all day. Then I got a mischievous thought. Sometimes I do that. Not often, but once in a while.

What would happen if I gave one of them a touch of the dazzle—not much, just one millionth of one percent and see what happens.

You know the dazzle, the spark, just a smidgen of what I have, only very watered down.

(SHE holds her chin, smiling and thinking.)

(SHE stops and hesitantly pokes her forefinger at the globe.)

Oh what the hell!

(The stage goes dark. Lightning and thunder are heard. A spotlight illuminates a spot on the stage. The gardener goes hesitantly toward the spotlight as if examining the globe.)

Maybe I should have just kept it as a bland mud ball.

Oh well, it's done now.

(SHE picks up her hoe and begins to walk off stage. She stops and turns toward the spotlight.)

I'll be back. When I come back to tidy up the garden I'll check it and see how this thing is doing. It should be worth a giggle or two.

January, 2010

COURAGE

Courage my son,
You are about to fall
Not once
But many times
Through twisted themes
And blackened dreams
That beat you
'til you're raw
Pick up again
Stand alone
Spit it from your craw
To fall again
To ache again
But to rise again
Once more

October, 1970

Was Jenny Here?

Was Jenny here
another year
when lights were
soft and warm?

Did she sit
once there
an empty chair
a lonely room
some place
somewhere?

Was Jenny here?
No, I fear
she really
wasn't here
at all.

May, 1969

CLUTTERED ATTIC

Between my ears
Through the years
A cluttered attic
Lies
Soot and dust
Cover booty
Plundered with
My eyes

Wispy things
Gossamer wings
Lie there
Fast asleep

A mother's sigh
A baby's cry
Are scattered
In a heap

Love's first flush
A tiny blush
Rest happily
Alone

February, 2006

MY BACK, IT CREAKS

My body has betrayed me
A bird chirps in my ear
My bladder leaks
My back it creaks
My eyesight fades each year
But still, I'm sure
I can bear it all
As long
As I'm
Still here

March, 2006

Lost Love

It came
during the winter
of my soul
feathers
soft as down
and
as I held it
in a firm
but gentle hand
and
heard it sing
a high sweet
simple song
a voice said
"Let it be."
It will live
again
but only in
your dreams
And it did

Summer, 1969

No Big Hollywood Ending: Part 1

We all knew he was going to die. It was just that we didn't know when. I mean, the doctor at the home kept saying he had only a few days to live, but he kept hanging in there, day after day, tough old bird. But that's the way they made them back then.

He'd had a stroke nine months earlier that had paralyzed his left side, and he couldn't pronounce words anymore. He tried, but they all came out, "Eh-h-h, eh-h-h" or "u-u-u-n-n-n-n-n." He'd throw up his hands in frustration, roll his eyes and move his head from side to side.

We brought him home for Thanksgiving dinner, because we thought it would cheer him up. Big mistake: he thought he was coming home to stay. At the end of the day, when we returned him to his wheelchair to take him back to the home, he raged silently. Beating my arm with his one good hand. He continued this during the ride back—staring at me with contempt in his eyes and mumbling as loud as he could, "u-u-n-n-n-, u-u-n-n." I still feel those weak blows today.

October, 1972

Home

Hi God. It's me.

It's good to see you again. How are you?

OK, I guess. Just a little confused.

What confuses you, my son?

Well, what was it all about?

What do you remember?

Let's see—I was born.

You mean you left me.

Yes, I guess so. But I don't remember that. I only started to remember things when I was four or five years old.

All according to plan.

Then things went so fast, like the blink of an eye. I grew, I went to school, got a job. Had three kids. Then I got old, had grandkids, got sick and died.

No, ... No. You came back to me.

But I still don't know what it was all about. What did it mean? What was I supposed to do? I never knew.

Oh, I think you always knew. It just took a little time for you to finally realize it.

Could it be, that it was all about trying to find my way back to you?

(God smiles broadly)

Well, let's put it this way, it's good to have you home again.

(End)

February, 2009

The God Man
PART I

Mathew Mathias found out he was God at 3:00 on a Friday morning. The voice sounded thin and raspy. But the message was very clear.

"You are the Messiah," it said. You are Almighty God—come to save the world."

"Isn't that weird?" he said to his friend, Rocky, the next day on their usual Saturday fishing excursion.

"And you don't even go to church," laughed Rocky.

"But I do watch Jimmy Recketts every Sunday."

Rocky laughed again. "I don't think watching a TV evangelist once a week qualifies as going to church."

That night, he had the dream once more. He watched Jimmy Recketts the next day, waiting impatiently for the 800 contact number to appear.

When it did, he called immediately and the first miracle occurred.

Not only would Jimmy Recketts see him; he wanted an appointment set up right away.

"How old are you?" Asked Recketts. "Thirty," responded Matt.

"And what do you do for a living?"

"I work for the Vermont Maplewood Furniture Company building wood cabinets."

"You're a carpenter?"

"So to speak."

"And you're single, right?"

"Yes."

Recketts rose from his chair, picked up a silver pen from the desk and began to tap his front teeth with it. Deep in thought, he paced back and forth very slowly.

He stopped, looked up, and shouted: "It fits. It all fits. You're him...returned to finish his ministry."

"And is this what you believe?"

Recketts replied: "Hardly, I believe you're a guy who had a strange dream, that's all. But the important thing is, you fit the description of the Messiah perfectly. And we are going to make that work for us."

The Recketts publicity machine went into high gear the very next day.

Press release headlines said:

MASTER MATHIAS TO APPEAR ON JIMMY RECKETTS SHOW.
THE SECOND COMING
DIVINE REVELATION

The great night arrived with all the pomp of a Super Bowl half-time show. Radio City Music Hall was rented. And the people responded: every seat was taken. The lines snaked down 6th Avenue and surrounding streets for blocks.

Jimmy Recketts stood on stage, a single bright spot illuminating his face. He said one sentence: "And now may I present the soon-to-be renowned Master Mathias."

The great curtain parted to reveal a slight man dressed in white monk's robes. He stepped into the spotlight and raised his hands to quiet the thunderous applause.

And then began a sermon that nobody wanted to hear. It seemed to offend all the power brokers in the world.

All weapons must be confiscated and destroyed.

All religious institutions must be abolished.

There will be only one church and that will be founded on principles set forth by Master Mathias.

All conflicts between God's creatures must cease immediately.

All disputes will reach peaceful resolution at a special international tribunal.

And so on, and so on.

The very next day an emergency session of the council of Christian Bishops was called to deal with the situation.

The NRA summoned top-level members to attend a special meeting of their top-secret disaster committee.

Certain members of an elite Navy Seal group were called to CIA Headquarters in Washington.

The IRS called a meeting of its special investigating unit.

They all had one question: What can we do to neutralize this dangerous man?

While the debate continued, the money poured in for Mathias' ministry.

Jimmy Recketts called Mathias to a meeting in his office. Recketts had a huge smile on his face as Mathias sat in a chair opposite him. "So, you're a huge success. The money is pouring in. Have you thought about what you're going to do with it all?"

Mathias appeared flustered. He moved his head slowly from side to side in a bewildered motion. "I don't know. It's all so unexpected."

"Well I know. So I've hired a money manager for you. And the first thing you do is settle your account with Jimmy Recketts' TV Production."

"Account? What account?"

"You know, the paper you signed. You didn't read it, did you? You owe us 65% of any monies you acquired after your TV appearance."

"Wow! 65%, I didn't know."

"Well, now you do." Said Jimmy. "Welcome to the real world, God-man. And by the way, if you read the contract further down it says that the rest of the money will be used to build the new Mathias gold cathedral."

Mathias grinned. "I shudder to ask. And what do I do with a gold-plated church?"

"Live in it. Conduct your ministry sessions in the great hall."

"The great hall?"

"You've never seen anything like it. Magnificent. Awe inspiring. I run out of words to describe it. And, by the way, I designed it myself."

"I can't believe you would run out of words for anything."

"Look, Matt, I've liked you from the start. You're a good guy. I'm sorry that I had to pull a couple of fast ones on you. But this is business. Sometimes I win, sometimes you do. But it all evens out in the end."

The two men stood up. After a few moments, staring silently at one another, Recketts offered his hand.

"Let bygones be bygones and move on. We still have a lot more money to be made."

"Come on, shake." He thrust his hand closer to Matt. "Let's have a drink on it."

He looked around the desk. On a tray with two glasses stood a water pitcher. He reached over, grabbed the tray and put it in front of him. He poured a glass of water and put in in front of Matt.

"Sorry, we only have water on hand to celebrate—but next time—champagne!"

Matt looked at him intently and pointed to the water pitcher. "May I have that?" he asked.

Recketts smiled from ear to ear. "You want to pour one for me?" Matt nodded ascent. "Sure buddy, sure you can."

Matt reached over, picked up the pitcher and remaining glass and poured the liquid into it.

Without looking up Recketts picked up the glass and downed it in one gulp. "See, nothing to it, now we can be ......"

Suddenly, Recketts grabbed his throat and began to cough loudly. His face turned red and his eyes bulged almost out of their sockets. Still holding the glass, he pointed his index finger at Mathias and screamed.

"You changed it to...."

Mathias calmly removed the glass from his hand and placed it on the desk.

"To what Jimmy? To what?"

"To....to <u>wine</u>."

The God-man smiled.

"Now, I think you understand."

PART II

The following week the Jimmy Recketts TV Production Company was destroyed, or to be more accurate, it imploded. And then Jimmy Recketts himself did something he had never done in his entire life—<u>he</u> <u>became</u> <u>a</u> <u>follower</u>.

On the Monday after his meeting with Mathias, Recketts dissolved his TV Production company.

On Tuesday, he announced he was devoting the rest of his life to helping Master Mathias achieve the goals of his ministry.

And the following week he began construction on the golden cathedral on the hill.

His goal—full completion of the church within three months. The site was to be on a high-rise tract of land just outside of Los Angeles.

The Mathias phenomenon had begun. Within months hundreds of thousands of members joined the new group.

Money followed in like a giant tidal wave. Dollars swept across the nation and into the coffers of the Golden Church.

But black clouds were forming: For every follower he attracted, Mathias gathered an equal number of enemies, each dedicated to his demise.

Seated on a bench in beautiful Rock Creek Park in Washington D.C., a tall lanky man neatly attired in a black Brooks Brothers suit, was speaking softly to a stocky blonde-haired companion seated next to him. The man had a crew haircut and a deep red gash across his right cheek.

The blonde-haired man had been summoned to a job interview with a secret Government agency, to be conducted in a place where no one could see or hear them.

The interviewee was Henry Judea, a small time crook, con man and mauler who, for a price, would "solve" problems the agency had that would be too distasteful for them to correct themselves.

The subject at the moment was money.

"I figure $20,000 in silver certificates should cover your payment," said the Brooks Brothers suit.

Judea winced.

"I think $30,000 would be more like it. You're asking me to mess this guy up and 'off him' if necessary."

"We never said that," retorted the government man.

"$30,000 or I walk."

The government man hung his head for a moment and then raised it abruptly.

"Okay, $30,000. But it better be done right."

"Whatever that means," grunted Judea.

Meanwhile, the cathedral was completed in less than 2-1/2 months.

Mathias spoke on a weekly basis in the great hall at the TV times originally slated for Jimmy Recketts. And more new disciples flocked to his ministry.

One of the new followers applied for a maintenance job at the new church. On his job application under "special talents," he wrote "fixer."

His name was Henry Judea.

Mathias did not like the gold church. He much preferred preaching to the overflow crowds on the beautiful green hill behind the edifice.

But he stayed there at night in a small apartment in the rear of the cathedral, spending most of his time praying for guidance and working in a large office library next to his bedroom.

During the day he roamed the poor section of LA with his good friend, Rocky, handing out food and medicine to those in need. And tending to the sick.

Within a few weeks, he began to be followed by reporters from all the local TV and radio outlets. Most had cameras and <u>all</u> had questions.

"Are you really the savior? If you are here to relieve the misery of the common folk why don't you wave your hand and let food and meds fall from the heavens?"

"Are you invincible like Superman? Can bullets kill you? Can you fly?"

"Is Mathias your real name? If you're Jesus why don't you say so?"

Mathias ignored them and went about his business. They crowded about him as he pushed his way through the narrow streets of Watts.

On one hot, steamy morning he turned to Rocky in frustration.

"Can't we lose these people?"

"Afraid not Matt. You've gotten big now and everyone wants a piece of you."

Mathias grinned in acknowledgement. "And I guess that's the way it should be."

A thin black man in a tattered T-shirt muscled his way through the mob and then to Mathias' side. He grabbed his arm in a vise-like grip.

"Hey man! Man!" he shouted. "You godda help me! It's my kid. He's bad sick. I think he's dying."

Mathias rested his arm in a gentle hug about the man's waist.

"Certainly," he said quietly, "where is he?"

The thin man pointed and Mathias followed.

He bent over, put his lips close to the man's ear and whispered "What's his name?"

"Lawrence" was the reply. "But we call him Larry."

Mathias grinned and said, "I know him."

The black man had no idea what that meant. His main concern was to lead the man to the basement door of a small apartment. When Matt entered the musty room, the acrid smell stopped him cold. There on a urine stained couch lay a 14-year-old boy groaning in pain. His eyes were closed and great beads of sweat poured down his face and onto his drenched upper torso.

Mathias knelt beside him and gripped his free hand. "I'm here son, I'm here." The boy feebly raised his eyelids.

"I know, I know. I've been waiting for you." He closed his eyes and fell into a deep coma.

After a few moments, Matt rose and turned to the boy's father.

"He's at peace for the moment. I'll return tomorrow to see what more can be done."

The old man wailed and cried loudly.

"He was my first and only son. And now I've lost him. First his mother and now him."

He fell into Mathias' arms crying in short, fearful sobs.

"Be strong. We'll see what we can do tomorrow," said Matt.

Mathias rose up and left the room.

During the night the boy died. When Mathias returned the next day he had trouble making his way through the throngs of media people, curiosity seekers and believers.

With Rocky's help, Mathias arrived at the front door. It opened, but before entering he turned to the shouting crowd and said, "Have you no shame? Stay away from this place, this boy is in the hands of God, God will determine what needs to be done. Pray. Pray and be silent."

He entered the apartment and slammed the door behind him. The door remained closed through the morning and into the afternoon. It was during the early mists of the evening that the front door finally creaked open.

An emaciated, wide-eyed black man staggered into the dark alleyway.

"He's alive! He's alive!" he cried, "Come back from the dead. All praise to the Master."

A hush fell over the throng.

When Mathias appeared in the doorway, a great cacophony of sound boomed down the alleyway and roared through the east section of Watts.

Mathias stepped into the moonlight and raised both arms. Within seconds, there was total silence.

Mathias' voice rose above the multitudes.

"I have come to comfort the poor, the weak, the powerless. Come, follow me, I have come to teach you how to love one another."

Someone took a video and within hours, the image of the man in the doorway in a white monk's cowl went viral.

PART III

The aftermath of the incident in Watts hit the LA area like a thunderbolt.

From all over the world came inquiries about Master Mathias and his new church. Requests for interviews from the international press poured in.

New believers stormed the web looking for hotel, motel or B&B accommodations in the LA area so they could come to hear Mathias in person.

The following Sunday the crush of people was so huge that the Great Hall could only handle half of them.

A second TV appearance was scheduled for Wednesday evening. The program was moved from the Great Hall to the slopes behind the church.

Enormous loudspeakers were set up on the crest of the hill, flanking a large platform. Klieg light were installed. The entire area was bathed in an eerie whitish grey glow that gave the rolling fields another worldly appearance.

Spotlights were strategically placed so when Mathias appeared, his was the only face to capture the light out of the darkness.

The commotion prompted a meeting with Mathias with the LA Chief of Police and a ranking member of the city council. They were very polite.

"We understand that you are a holy man and are dedicated to spread your gospel," said the chief. "Unfortunately, your random forays into the city are causing us a great deal of trouble."

"What kind of trouble?" asked Mathias quietly.

"Traffic jams, work stoppages and general unrest," said the council member.

"What would you have me do?"

"Please do not leave the compound without first letting us know. We will provide police officers to protect you."

Mathias waved his hand dismissively. "I don't believe I need them. With 12 of my very best disciples who follow me at all times, I'm sure I'll be safe."

"We don't think so. So bear with us. We're professionals in crowd control."

"To sum up," said the council member, "We would prefer you remain in your church, give your bi-weekly sermons there, and venture out as little as possible."

Mathias rose from the table where he was seated. "I will do my best to abide by your requests.

"Now I have work to do, and **very little time to do it**."

Mathias repeated this to his followers at their weekly supper. "Why do you tell us this," they chimed in, puzzled. "But you are such a young, vital man. Your work will go on for years."

He looked around the table, and in a sad voice said, "I am with you in spirit forever. But the flesh will die shortly."

The disciples were restive. They had no idea what this meant.

"Are you dying of some disease, Lord?"

"No, but this world we are trying to save is already dying of terrible diseases—envy, greed, hatred. And one of these diseases is going to put an end to me. Soon."

PART IV

Mathias kept his word for five weeks. He stayed in the gold church during the day and was seen only on television two times a week.

It didn't stop the amazing financial growth of his new organization. But he became restless and felt the need to be personally among his followers.

One night he donned a beard and mustache that he found in a backstage dressing room at the old Recketts Production Company.

Donning a large black robe he found in the wardrobe department, he put on his facial disguise and ventured out into nearby Watts; at first once a week and then two and three nights every several days.

On one excursion, he became lost on his way home. He entered a narrow walkway between two large buildings and was moving rapidly, his path lighted up by the yellow-orange glow that the moon cast on the pathway before him.

Mathias paused thinking he heard the sound of heavy breathing coming from one of the doorways. Suddenly, a powerful arm reached out of the blackness and imprisoned his head in a bear-like grip. Then the beating began. A large hammer-like fist plunged into his side. Another blow struck his ribs, cracking two of them. Mathias could barely breathe and he pulled at the assaillant's arm trying to free himself.

The mauling stopped for a moment as the brute twirled him around and then slammed a fist into his face. Mathias fell to the ground. A great moan came from Mathias' lips as he fell on his hands and knees. His robe parted showing small red blood spots on his white tunic.

The beast hovered above him and in a high pitched raspy voice shouted, "Just a little lesson for now! Stop what you're doing or the next time you'll never get up."

Mathias looked up from his kneeling position and glanced at the brute towering over him. His face was silhouetted against the moonlit sky and Mathias' brief look at him captured a blonde haired man with a deep red gash across his face. He had seen this man before.

The mugger moved forward quickly and gave his victim a swift kick to his side. Then he paused, turned abruptly and raced from the scene, disappearing into the murky darkness.

"It's a wonder you're still alive," said the nurse later at the infirmary inside the gold church. "You should be out of commission for at least two weeks!"

The doctor who was called later reiterated the nurse's diagnosis. "You'll need plenty of rest, so for right now I'll give you a sedative to help that."

Re-runs of his previous performances were aired on Sundays and Wednesdays for the following two weeks.

The announcement from Recketts television production said, "Master Mathias has suffered a severe fall from a ladder and he will be laid up for two weeks while he recuperates. He welcomes your prayers."

Prayers were offered for his recovery throughout the world, twenty-four hours a day.

His disciples were shocked and feared for his life thinking that this was his prophecy come true. But Mathias reassured them from his hospital bed that his time had not come—at least not for now.

Mathias was up and around within a week and a half, confounding the doctor and his followers as well as generating talk of another miracle. Mathias' bright, happy face appeared on television the following Sunday to the delight of his friends and followers.

It was announced that Master Mathias, with the help of prayers and a divine spiritual power, would resume his regularly scheduled TV appearances.

His nighttime ventures ceased immediately. And things returned to normal, or so it seemed.

Mathias' recovery was nothing short of miraculous. Within weeks, the puffiness around his eyes had disappeared and the black eye was gone. Dark red bruises around his body had given way to greyish-green scabs and dark skin.

The only reminder of the cruel beating was the cast set about his ribs and this was slated to be removed shortly.

Mathias had a triumphant return to his TV pulpit and things went on as before. Then one night in his chambers, that all changed radically. A hospital bed had been rolled into his bedroom to help him rest comfortably. It didn't help with his brain. His nighttime slumbers were constantly plagued by vivid terror dreams. He woke up several times a night convinced he was still back in that dismal alleyway.

One night he awoke with a start. Something was wrong. He looked around the room in the dark. Nothing was out of place. No strange noises—or were there? His deeply sensitive eardrums picked up the soft sound of papers being shuffled—indistinct but there nonetheless. His eyes slowly became used to the blackness and he moved his head ever so slowly from left to right and then back again—then he saw it.

A tiny speck of light glowed sporadically along the bottom crack of the door jamb leading to his office. He pushed his covers aside, stepped out of bed and tiptoed gingerly to the door. The sound was much more audible now. The short bursts of light continued to pierce the bottom door jamb. He pressed his body full length to the door and held his breath.

Abruptly it came to him—somebody was shuffling papers on his desk. He undoubtedly had a flashlight gripped in his teeth which jerked around as he folded papers with his hands.

He threw the door open and turned on the light.

There, stooped over the desk was a figure he recognized immediately. The bulky, muscle armed, blonde crew cut with the vicious gash down his right cheek. It was Judea dressed in canvas workman's coveralls with a small flashlight gripped in his mouth. He was leafing through folders, glancing up casually he smiled at Mathias.

"Sorry I wakened you. I should have been more quiet."

"What are you doing here?" said Mathias angrily.

Judea stopped. He paused for a moment, titled his head back and emitted a hideous laugh.

"You mean you didn't get it after the beating I gave you? I'm here to mess you up. I'm looking for something we can use to screw up your name and turn you from the God Man into maybe something evil."

Mathias advanced toward the desk.

"Hold it pal," said Judea. "I don't want to waste you now. It's not in the plan. So cool it."

Mathias reached the desk, his arms stretched out before him and said softly, "Judea, my son. Is the money you've gotten worth destroying me?"

Judea was startled. He pushed the desk chair away from the desk and stepped back a few feet. He then pulled a revolver from his waistband and pointed it at Mathias. His voice quivered when he spoke.

"How do you know my name? Where do you come from?"

Mathias put his hands on the desk and pleaded with him.

"Don't do this. Come follow me. I'm here to save you."

Judea pressed his back against the wall and steadied the revolver with his other hand.

"You're a devil! A devil! Go away!" he screamed.

He pressed the trigger of the revolver and the bullet leaped out and sped toward Mathias' head—it passed by inches, hit the side door of a steel safe and ricocheted back over the desk and into Judea's right eye penetrating his brain. He dropped like a dead weight onto the floor and then rolled over.

Mathias rushed to his side. He gently removed the gun from Judea's hand and placed it on the floor next to the body. He knelt on one knee and began to pray in a loud voice.

He was still praying when the police arrived some time later.

"Impossible," said Will Gerwin (22 years on the L.A. Police Force). He was sitting in Mathias' library just after listening to Mathias' recounting of his story.

"This guy breaks into the Master's office looking to steal something. Mathias surprises him and then this guy shoots at him. And what happens? The bullet misses Mathias' head, hits a steel safe and then ricochets in a straight line and buries itself into the burglar's brain. You expect me to believe that?"

Gerwin slapped the top of his head and growled.

"Come off it! Tell me what really happened."

Gerwin put his face as close as he could to Mathias. "You knew this guy, didn't you?"

Mathias hesitated and then with a deep sigh, said "yes, I did."

Gerwin rushed in for the kill.

"As a matter of fact, he was the one who beat you up in Watts a month ago, wasn't he? You wonder how I know about this confidential police report made at the hospital that night?"

"How can anyone believe this cock-and-bull story of a bouncing bullet that miraculously comes to rest in a burglar's eye?"

Gerwin whirled around and addressed the other cops in the room.

"Want to know what really happened? You sneaked out in the middle of the night about a month ago not to minister to your flock. You had other things in mind, but I'll get to that. You found this guy, got beat up so bad you were put in the hospital. You found out that he was a maintenance man at your church and decided to take revenge. You then got him to come to your office on the pretext of needing his help to repair something. Then after he came, you got the drop on him and killed him."

"Nice story," said Mathias "but why would I call him to come in the middle of the night to discuss a repair?"

"I said I was coming to that," said Gerwin.

"Remember the beating you got in Watts? How come you sneaked out at night when you were told by the police to stay at the church? Why were you so compelled to do this dangerous thing? <u>Was it lust</u>? Were you looking for men— soliciting them for sex? This guy probably resented you for approaching him and beat the hell out of you. He didn't know why you asked him to come to your room. I suspect it was out of lust first and then revenge."

Mathias glared at him.

"That's pretty far-fetched."

"Is it?" asked Gerwin. "We just got a preliminary report from the fingerprint lab and your prints are on the murder weapon. What have you got to say about that?"

Mathias started to reply but Gerwin stopped him. He reached to the back of his belt saying as he did, "Mathew Mathias, I'm arresting you on suspicion of the murder of Henry Judea." He produced handcuffs and snapped them onto Matt's wrists.

"And in case you didn't know, the penalty for murder in this state is death by hanging."

PART V

Judge Carleton L. Fister was the splitting image of Abraham Lincoln, except for his nose. The proboscis had been broken when he was thirteen years old. It was hit by an errant baseball in a little league game. The nose twisted torturously down the front of his face, ending at two blue-red lips just above his jaw. But the rest of his image held to the Lincoln description; a shock of black hair, high angular cheekbones and piercing eyes set deep in their sockets.

The lamp on his desk shed light only on the bottom half of his face, giving his eyes a sinister look.

He was listening to a dark man seated across the desk from him. A man whom he disliked intensely. The fellow was speaking in a demanding tone, occasionally poking his index finger on the judge's desk when he needed emphasis on a point.

"What an irksome creature," thought Fister, "where do they get these people?"

"We want this to move fast," said the man, "through the Grand Jury and onto trial quickly—and most importantly, we need a guilty verdict."

Fister leaned back in his adjustable seat, propped his elbows on the arms and spidered his fingers.

"So, you want this man to disappear for a long time—say life?"

The man grinned.

"No, longer than that, in a word, <u>we want him dead!</u>"

The judge folded his arms and breathed deeply, trying to compose himself.

"You can't be serious," he said in a deep whisper.

"Oh, we're serious judge. And you'd better be too. You know we have a way to persuade you to do this. But we would prefer not to use that on such a distinguished gentleman like yourself."

"So that was it," thought Fister. "They're going to use it on me, the one thing that could shatter my career and probably my life." He winced, then leaning forward, he placed his elbows on the desk and put his face into his hands. "Okay," he said sadly, "but the prosecutor will have to pick the right people for the jury or this won't fly."

"Got it," said the lackey for the power brokers. "Thank you, Your Honor. It's a pleasure doing business with you."

After the man left, Fister ran to his personal bathroom and vomited into the toilet.

Like a hot knife through butter, the case raced swiftly through the L.A. judicial system. Within weeks an indictment was put forward and by the end of the month, a date was set for the trial. The trial judge? The honorable Carleton L. Fister.

Lionel M. Poindexter, the D.A. for Los Angeles county was known as a specialist in handling tough murder indictments. He was positive he could get a guilty verdict in this case given the evidence he had.

As he approached the bench he had a smile on his face and he walked in a grim, determined manner. He began his opening statement.

"What we have here, Your Honor, is a fairytale where the so-called facts to be presented by the defense are really suppositions and in reality, are no more than the imaginings of a corrupt mind. Make no mistake about it. Mathew Mathias is a corrupt individual. He claimed to be inspired by a voice he heard in the middle of the night that said he was *the Messiah*."

"His first thought was how to make money on this. So he contacted the evangelist, Jimmy Recketts, and appeared on his weekly T.V. program. And get this—the public believed him! The money rolled in, so much so that he was able to build a golden church on a hill outside of L.A. But this hoaxter had a big problem—his sexual orientation. He's gay."

"Now, I have nothing against gay people. Some of my best friends are gay. But his lust was insatiable!"

Poindexter paused to make the moment more dramatic.

"So in the dark of night he prowled the streets of Watts looking for unsuspecting young men to solicit. He met one that rebuffed his advances and gave him a sound thrashing."

"Later, when Mathias found out he was a maintenance man at his own church he decided to lure this man to his chambers. First to attempt a second seduction but more likely for the purpose of revenge."

"Now the accused will claim that he caught the man at night in his office trying to rob him. He says the victim pulled a gun and shot it at him at point blank range. Now, here's where it gets good. The bullet misses Mathias, who's only a few feet away, goes to the other end of the room, hits a safe door and ricochets in a line across the room and hits Judea right in his brain. Nice shot!"

"And we will hear from the defense the most ridiculous claim of them all. That after Judea fell to the floor, Mathias kneeled down to pray for him and in so doing, removed the gun from his hand and placed it on the floor next to the body."

"I leave it to you, Judge, how can anyone believe this kind of malarkey? The State intends to prove Mathew Mathias, the so-called, Master, planned the death of Henry

Judea to avenge a beating. This charlatan, this killer, needs to be removed from our society and severely punished for his deeds as prescribed by the laws for premediated murder in this State."

"Your Honor, I thank you for your attention and patience."

The D.A. strode back to his chair; a contented smirk on his face.

PART VI

Against the advice of some of his followers who were lawyers, Mathias decided to act in his own defense.

Therefore, it was he who approached the bench to give his opening statement. The judge spent most of his time scribbling in a small spiral bound notebook.

Mathias turned to the side and addressed the crowd in the courtroom and the T.V. camera. Most of the address was spent reiterating the information he had given the police the night of the shooting.

He had gone out at night to visit the poor and the sick because going during the day would require police escorts and would probably result in huge crowds. Witnesses to his nighttime forays were mostly black and Hispanic. He could not call them to court because they feared the judicial system.

No, he didn't know why Judea beat him up. He said he was sending a message and that he was to stop doing what he was doing.

The subject of sex was immaterial since he was a-sexual, and had no interest in either men or women.

As far as the strange trajectory of the bullet, Mathias stopped talking. A huge grin began to spread across his face. He then laughed and spread his arms stretching them heavenwards.

"Thank you, Father."

Judge Fister moved the trail along in a brisk fashion. He knew how to cut corners without making it look like he was prejudiced to the Defense. He was aided by, of all people; Mathias himself.

During a trial recess, Rocky confronted him.

"Matt, what are you doing? You're helping them send you to the gallows. You know this whole thing is a setup. You stepped on too many toes. You are being good and righteous, but all they can see is a hit to their pocketbooks."

Rocky stood across from the table from where Matt sat, his hands folded and his head down.

"Thank you for your concern, Rock. But this is proceeding according to plan. It is preordained and I will help it to proceed as rapidly as possible."

Rocky was astonished. "You planned everything to make it come out this way?"

"Yes, with the Father. We needed to reaffirm the nature of the children that were created—that they have not gotten better, but worse. They have created the ability to destroy themselves with atomic bombs. With personal weapons they slay one another in the name of the creator. Greed. Envy. Hate. Prejudice. No concern for their immortal souls but only with their transient bodies. So I came once more to shed my blood for their sins."

Mathias stood up, walked to Rocky and put both hands on his shoulders.

"But now my time grows short. I have some important things to discuss."

Mathias' eyes burned into Rocky's as he spoke. "My wonderful friend, I will be leaving you shortly. And I need someone to carry on my work. I can think of no one better than you."

Rocky let out a great shout and fell to his knees. "No! No. No. No master. I can't do it." He gripped Matt around his knees and sobbed. Mathias lifted him up, put his arms around him and spoke in a voice full of surety.

"Of course you can, my friend. God will be with you every step of the way.

Guided by Judge Fister's practiced hand, the trial sped on. There was little evidence and few witnesses so the case came to its end in an unprecedented two and a half weeks. Fister came to his final decision late one night catching everyone by surprise. The T.V. newsmen who were staying at a nearby motel scrambled for their clothes and appeared totally disheveled in the courtroom.

Judge Fister strode in from a side door, his lips pursed tightly and a scowl on his face. He sat down, put on this spectacles and looked out over the courtroom.

A hush fell over the whole room. He pulled a folded piece of paper from inside his black robe, opened it and began to read.

"In the case of the State versus Mathew Mathias on the charge of murder in the first degree, I have deliberated long and hard and have come to the decision that the defendant is guilty of this charge."

Pandemonium broke out as reporters tried to leave their seats and rush out so they could give this news to their appropriate headquarters.

Judge Fister raised his hand to quiet the crowd. He banged his gavel several times and in a loud voice said, "Return to your seats. There's more. THERE'S MORE!"

A loud shuffling noise could be heard as the reporters returned to their chairs.

The judge continued.

"For a cold-blooded, planned murder such as this was, there can be only one decision. The defendant must pay the ultimate price for this heinous crime—death by hanging."

The judge's final words were drowned out by a tumultuous roar from the courtroom crowd.

"Mathew Mathias, it is the ruling of this court that you be taken to the State penitentiary where in exactly one month from now you will be hanged by the neck until you are dead."

The following month passed slowly as thousands pressed the jail officials to visit the Master one last time.

Jimmy Recketts talked to Mathias for almost one hour offering his T.V. facilities for use by his followers. Rocky spent every day in the cell with him making plans for future meetings in his name.

A young man named Larry fell to his knees when he entered the cell. He kissed Matt's feet and sobbed and then thanked the Master for his life. When a thin, bony black man came in he grasped his hand with Mathias' intertwining them and prayed aloud for a full hour.

The day before the hanging Mathias had the strangest visitor of all. An ashen faced Judge Fister came into his cell. Fister could not look Mathias in the face but instead peered out the barred top window as he spoke.

His voice quivered throughout his discourse.

"It was brought to my attention just yesterday that the man who was killed was an agent at a secret government agency hired with the sole purpose of destroying you—either by beatings or if necessary, by killing you. With this new information it is necessary that I put aside the verdict and call for a new trial. It will be difficult but with my influence, I think it can be done."

Mathias placed his hands on Fister's shoulders and spoke quietly. "Please son, I know you were in on the conspiracy and I know how you were forced to do it."

Fister whirled around and confronted him. "How would you know about that?

Mathias grinned.

Certainly he knew about the under-aged girl that Fister had slept with and how the power brokers used it to blackmail him when needed.

"But I do know. I've know it all along."

Fister fell into Mathias' arms crying.

"It will not be necessary to retry me. I was destined to end my life like this, with or without your help."

Mathias hugged Fister for a long time before releasing him. He looked at him for the last time and said his final words.

"Go now, my son. I forgive you."

Mathias approached the noose and stood before it while the hangman fitted it around his neck. The hangman fell to his knees and tears rolled down his face. "Forgive me Master," he sobbed. Mathias touched the top of his head and whispered in his ear, "you have already been forgiven, my son."

Mathias turned to the watching crowd and said his last words.

"Death has never stopped me before and it will not stop me now. I will return once again but next time, I will bring eternal salvation for all my children."

He raised both hands. "Bless you. And I love you ALL!"

The lever was pulled and Mathias' body fell through the trapdoor.

For years to come, his followers wore silver neckbands the bottom of which depicted a tiny noose with a torn rope above it.

THE END

2013

www.ingramcontent.com/pod-product-compliance
Lightning Source LLC
Chambersburg PA
CBHW020604130626
46552CB00007B/3033